Across State Lines

America's 50 States
as Represented in Poetry

EDITED BY

THE AMERICAN POETRY & LITERACY PROJECT

DOVER PUBLICATIONS, INC.
Mineola, New York

EDITORS OF THIS VOLUME
ROBBIE SPILKA KLEIN
ANDREW CARROLL

ASSOCIATE EDITORS
GEORGE DANIEL PATTERSON
HENRY LABALME
ELIZABETH ELAM ROTH

Dedicated to the memory of Patricia H. Labalme
1927–2002

Bibliographical Note

Across State Lines: America's 50 States as Represented in Poetry, first published in 2003, is a new selection of poems published for The American Poetry & Literacy Project by Dover Publications, Inc., Mineola, New York.

Library of Congress Cataloging-in-Publication Data

Across state lines : America's 50 States as Represented in Poetry / edited by the American Poetry & Literacy Project.
    p. cm.
  Includes index.
  ISBN 0-486-42859-1 (pbk.)
  1. American poetry. 2. U.S. states—Poetry. I. American Poetry & Literacy Project (Mineola, N.Y.)
PS595.U5A625 2003
811'.608—dc21

2002041723

Manufactured in the United States of America
Dover Publications, Inc., 31 East 2nd Street, Mineola, N.Y. 11501

On Journeys Through the States

"I readily admit that the Americans have no poets," Alexis de Tocqueville famously remarked in *Democracy in America*, his acclaimed 19th century critique of this nation. "Nothing conceivable is so petty, so insipid, so crowded with paltry interests—in one word, so anti-poetic—as the life of a man in the United States."

While Tocqueville saw a country with no ancient legends to draw upon, no accounts of royal intrigue to chronicle, and no epic tales or myths to re-fashion, American writers looked out over the vastness of the land and its varied cast of citizens and found inspiration wherever they looked. "The Americans of all nations at any time upon the earth have probably the fullest poetical nature," proclaimed Walt Whitman, a contemporary of Tocqueville. "The United States themselves are essentially the greatest poem."

The poems in this collection demonstrate the profound influence this country has had—and continues to have—on its writers. Individually, however, the works featured here are not about America. Rather, each poem is about or relates to in some way a specific state (and Washington, D.C.). Some poems reference their state prominently, others do so more peripherally. Some are written by natives, others by new residents or travelers just passing through. Each state is represented by at least one poem, but the three most populous— California, New York, and Texas—are allowed a few more. Together, these more than fifty poems offer an impressionistic view of America, illuminating it from many perspectives and reflecting the colloquialisms and idiosyncracies of different regions.

No anthology can capture all of the characteristics, moods, and voices of an entire nation—and certainly not one as sprawling and diverse as the United States—but collectively the poems here convey a spirit of vitality, optimism, individuality, and adventurousness that is distinctly American. The latter, in particular, is one of the most recurring themes in this collection. United States history is one of expansion and exploration, and Americans' desire to roam and wander about the country has not diminished over time. Many of these poems describe short journeys, both literally through the states and more figuratively into the self, resulting in a kind of epiphany. For Tom Sexton it comes in Alaska as the autumn chill descends over the land, producing in the "querulous mind, the yearning heart/a sudden immeasurable calm." For James Wright it occurs while driving through Minnesota, when a serendipitous encounter feeding two Indian ponies overwhelms him with such happiness, he remarks: "[I]f I stepped out of my body I would break/Into blossom." For Joyce Carol Oates it happens on I-95 heading into New Jersey. For Hayden Carruth it's in Vermont, for Nikki Giovanni in the city of New York, and for Miller Williams it comes at a traffic light in Fayetteville, Arkansas. The poets are transformed by what they observe and feel in these places, and they invite us all to share in the experience.

America is not of course without its imperfections, and these poems do not shy away from revealing its darker corners. "They tell me you are wicked and I believe them for I have seen/your painted women under the gas lamps luring the farm boys," Carl Sandburg writes of Chicago, Illinois. In his 1940 poem "Daybreak in Alabama," Langston Hughes envisions Alabama as he would like to see it—not only with its remarkable natural beauty, but free of prejudice, with "black hands and brown and yellow hands" working together. As beautiful as America is, these poets remind us, it is still a work in progress.

But at the heart of this collection, even within the poems that express words of ambivalence and criticism, there is a sentiment of deep affection for and kinship with the individual people and communities that constitute these fifty states. There is an implicit sense of being "home" wherever one travels and of sharing a common bond with those who, only moments before, were total strangers. And, because of the immensity and diversity of this country, there is an exhilaration in the endless opportunities for discovering new and sudden wonders. John Balaban articulates this best perhaps after a visit to Albuquerque, New Mexico. "At dusk, by the irrigation ditch/gurgling past backyards near the highway,/locusts raise a maze of calls in cottonwoods," he writes. "A Spanish girl in a white party dress/strolls the levees by the muddy water/where her small sister plunks in stones.../In the moment when the locusts pause and the girl/presses her up-fluttering dress to her bony knees/you can hear a banjo, guitar, and fiddle/playing 'The Mississippi Sawyer' inside a shack./Moments like that," Balaban concludes, "you can love this country."

—Robbie Spilka Klein
Andrew Carroll
The American Poetry & Literacy Project

Acknowledgments

Nan Arbuckle, "Grandfather's Song." Reprinted with the permission of Andrew Arbuckle.

John Balaban, "Passing through Albuquerque" from *Words for My Daughter*. Copyright © 1991 by John Balaban. Reprinted with the permission of Copper Canyon Press, P. O. Box 271, Port Townsend, WA 98368-0271.

Wendell Berry, "Kentucky River Junction" from *Collected Poems, 1957–1982*. Copyright © 1973 by Wendell Berry. Reprinted with the permission of North Point Press, a division of Farrar, Straus & Giroux, LLC.

Philip Booth, "Marin" from *Islanders*. Copyright © 1952, 1957, 1958, 1959, 1960, 1961 by Philip Booth. Reprinted with the permission of Viking Penguin, a division of Penguin Putnam Inc.

Fleda Brown, "A Few Lines from Rehoboth Beach" from *Do Not Peel the Birches*. Reprinted with the permission of the author and Purdue University Press.

Kathryn Stripling Byer, excerpt from "Mountain Time" from *Black Shawl*. Copyright © 1998 by Kathryn Stripling Byer. Reprinted with the permission of Louisiana State University Press.

Hayden Carruth, "The Cows at Night" from *From Snow and Rock, from Chaos*. Copyright © 1973 by Hayden Carruth. Reprinted with the permission of New Directions Publishing Corporation.

Willa Cather, "Prairie Spring" from *April Twilights and Other Poems*. Copyright 1933 by Willa Cather, renewed © 1961 by Edith Lewis and the City Bank Farmers Trust Company. Reprinted with the permission of Alfred A. Knopf, a division of Random House, Inc.

Tom Chandler, "Jerimoth Hill" from *Sad Jazz* (Table Rock Books, 2002). Reprinted with the permission of the author.

Lucille Clifton, "blessing the boats" from *Quilting: Poems 1987–1990*. Copyright © 1991 by Lucille Clifton. Reprinted with the permission of BOA Editions Ltd.

Billy Collins, "Fishing on the Susquehanna in July" from *Picnic, Lightning*. Copyright © 1998 by Billy Collins. Reprinted with the permission of the University of Pittsburgh Press.

Peggy Simson Curry, "Lupine Ridge" from *Red Wind of Wyoming, Third Edition* (Denver: Sage Books, 1955). Reprinted with the permission of the Estate of Peggy Simson Curry.

Harley Elliott, "Outside Abilene" from *The Minnesota Review*. Reprinted with the permission of the author.

Lawrence Ferlinghetti, "The Changing Light" from *How to Paint Sunlight*. Copyright © 2000 by Lawrence Ferlinghetti. Reprinted with the permission of New Directions Publishing Corporation. All rights reserved.

Robert Fitzgerald, "July in Indiana" from *Spring Shade*. Originally published in *The New Yorker*. Copyright © 1966 by Robert Fitzgerald. Reprinted with the permission of New Directions Publishing Corporation.

Roland Flint, "Early Cutting" from *And Morning* (Washington: Dryad Press, 1975). Copyright © 1975 by Roland Flint. Reprinted with the permission of the author.

Charles Foster, "How Everything Was in the End Resolved in California." Reprinted with the permission of Daleth Foster.

Robert Frost, "Stopping by Woods on a Snowy Evening" from *The Poetry of Robert Frost*, edited by Edward Connery Lathem. Copyright 1923, 1928 by Henry Holt and Company, Inc., renewed © 1951, 1956 by Robert Frost. Reprinted with the permission of the publishers.

Nikki Giovanni, "Just a New York Poem" from *My House*. Copyright © 1972 by Nikki Giovanni. Reprinted with the permission of HarperCollins Publishers, Inc.

Rebecca Gonzales, "South Texas Summer Rain" from *Slow Work to the Rhythm of Cicadas* (Fort Worth, Texas: Prickly Pear Press, 1985). Reprinted with the permission of the author.

Joseph Hansen, "Dakota: Five Times Six" from *The New Yorker Book of Poems* (New York: Morrow Quill, 1974). Reprinted with the permission of the author.

Edward L. Hart, "Spring" from *To Utah*. Copyright © 1979 by Brigham Young University Press. Reprinted by permission.

Daniel Whitehead Hicky, "Nocturne: Georgia Coast" from *The Saturday Evening Post* (1950). Copyright 1950 by Curtis Publishing Company. Reprinted by permission.

Langston Hughes, "Daybreak in Alabama" from *The Collected Poems of Langston Hughes*. Copyright 1936 and renewed © 1964 by Langston Hughes. Copyright © 1994 by the Estate of Langston Hughes. Reprinted with the permission of Alfred A. Knopf, a division of Random House, Inc.

Jane Kenyon, "At the Public Market Museum: Charleston, South

Carolina" from *Otherwise: New and Selected Poems*. Copyright ©
1996 by Jane Kenyon. Reprinted with the permission of Graywolf
Press, St. Paul, Minnesota.

Robert Kinsley, "A Walk Along the Old Tracks." from *Endangered
Species*. Copyright © 1998 by Robert Kinsley. Reprinted with the
permission of Orchises Press.

Robbie Spilka Klein, "Iowa." Reprinted with the permission of the author.

Juliet Kono, "Silverswords" from *Hilo Rains*. Copyright © 1988 by
Juliet Kono. Reprinted with permission.

Philip Levine, "Drum" from *The Mercy*. Copyright © 1999 by Philip
Levine. Reprinted with the permission of Alfred A. Knopf, a divi-
sion of Random House, Inc.

Janet Lewis, excerpt from "For John Muir, A Century and More After
His Time" from *The Selected Poems of Janet Lewis*. Copyright ©
2000. Reprinted with the permission of Ohio University
Press/Swallow Press.

Shirley Geok-lin Lim, "Seaweeds." Reprinted with the permission of
the author.

Amy Lowell, excerpt from "The Congressional Library" from *What's
O'Clock*. Copyright © 1955 by Houghton Mifflin Company,
Brinton P. Roberts and G. D'Andelot Belin, Esquire. Reprinted with
the permission of Houghton Mifflin Company. All rights reserved.

Walt McDonald, "The Waltz We Were Born For" from *Whatever the
Wind Delivers*. Copyright © 1999 by Texas Tech University Press.
Reprinted with the permission of the publishers.

Ron McFarland, "Idaho Requiem" from *Stranger in Town: New and
Selected Poems*. Copyright © 2000. Reprinted with the permission
of the author and Confluence Press.

Jeanne Mc Gahey, "Oregon Winter." Reprinted by permission.

N. Scott Momaday, "Earth and I Gave You Turquoise" from *The Gourd
Dancer* (New York: Harper & Row, 1975). Copyright © 1975 by
N. Scott Momaday. Reprinted with the permission of the author.

Howard Nemerov, "Found Poem" from *War Stories* (Chicago: The
University of Chicago Press, 1987). Copyright © 1987 by Howard
Nemerov. Reprinted with the permission of Margaret Nemerov.

Joyce Carol Oates, "Night Driving" from *The Time Traveler* (New York: E.
P. Dutton, 1989). Copyright © 1989 by Joyce Carol Oates. Reprinted
with the permission of Dutton, a division of Penguin Group (USA).

Mary Oliver, "Coming Home" from *Dream Work*. Copyright © 1986 by
Mary Oliver. Reprinted with the permission of Grove/Atlantic, Inc.

Michael Pettit, "Virginia Evening" from *Cardinal Points*. Copyright ©
1988 by Michael Pettit. Reprinted with the permission of
University of Iowa Press.

Kirk Robertson, "driving to Vegas" from *Driving to Vegas: New and Selected Poems 1969–1987* (Tucson: SUN/Gemini Press, 1989). Copyright © 1989 by Kirk Robertson. Reprinted with the permission of the author.

Carl Sandburg, "Chicago" from *Chicago*. Copyright 1916 by Holt Rinehart & Winston, Inc., renewed 1944 by Carl Sandburg. Reprinted with the permission of Harcourt, Inc.

George Scarbrough, "Tenantry." Reprinted with the permission of the author.

Tom Sexton, "Autumn in the Alaska Range" from *Autumn in the Alaska Range*. Copyright © 2000 by Tom Sexton. Reprinted with the permission of Salmon Publishing.

Gary Snyder, "Mid-August at Sourdough Mountain Lookout" from *Riprap*. Copyright © 1959 by Gary Snyder. Reprinted with the permission of North Point Press, a division of Farrar, Straus & Giroux, LLC.

William Stafford, "Once in the 40s" from *The Way It Is: New and Selected Poems*. Copyright © 1982, 1998 by the Estate of William Stafford. Reprinted with the permission of Graywolf Press, St. Paul, Minnesota.

Wallace Stevens, "Nomad Exquisite" from *Collected Poems*. Copyright © 1923, 1951, 1954 by Wallace Stevens. Reprinted with the permission of Alfred A. Knopf, a division of Random House, Inc.

Mark Van Doren, "The Hills of Little Cornwall" from *The Autobiography of Mark Van Doren*. Copyright © 1939, 1958, 1986. Reprinted with permission.

Robert Lewis Weeks, "Appalachian Front." Reprinted with the permission of Robin Weeks Pagliasotti.

Miller Williams, "Walking after Supper" from *Some Jazz A While: Collected Poems*. Copyright © 1989 by Miller Williams. Reprinted with the permission of the author and the University of Illinois Press.

James Wright, "A Blessing" from *The Branch Will Not Break*. Copyright © 1963 by James Wright. Reprinted with the permission of Wesleyan University Press.

The editors have taken all possible care to trace the ownership of poems under copyright in this book. If any errors or omissions have occurred, please contact the APL Project at: PO Box 53445, Washington, DC 20009, and any mistakes will be corrected.

Table of Contents

ALABAMA

Daybreak in Alabama

When I get to be a composer
I'm gonna write me some music about
Daybreak in Alabama
And I'm gonna put the purtiest songs in it
Rising out of the ground like a swamp mist
And falling out of heaven like soft dew.
I'm gonna put some tall tall trees in it
And the scent of pine needles
And the smell of red clay after rain
And long red necks
And poppy colored faces
And big brown arms
And the field daisy eyes
Of black and white black white black people
And I'm gonna put white hands
And black hands and brown and yellow hands
And red clay earth hands in it
Touching everybody with kind fingers
And touching each other natural as dew
In that dawn of music when I
Get to be a composer
And write about daybreak
In Alabama.

Langston Hughes

ALASKA

Autumn in the Alaska Range

Drive north when the braided glacial rivers
have begun to assume their winter green.
When crossing Broad Pass, you might see
the shimmer of caribou moving on a distant ridge
or find a dark abacus of berries in the frost
on the trail to Summit Lake. Beyond this,
the endless mountains curving like a scimitar.
And in the querulous mind, the yearning heart
a sudden immeasurable calm.

Tom Sexton

ARIZONA

Earth and I Gave You Turquoise

Earth and I gave you turquoise
    when you walked singing
We lived laughing in my house
    and told old stories
You grew ill when the owl cried
We will meet on Black Mountain

I will bring corn for planting
    and we will make fire
Children will come to your breast
    You will heal my heart
I speak your name many times
The wild cane remembers you

My young brother's house is filled
    I go there to sing
We have not spoken of you
    but our songs are sad
When Moon Woman goes to you
I will follow her white way

Tonight they dance near Chinle
    by the seven elms
There your loom whispered beauty
    They will eat mutton
and drink coffee till morning
You and I will not be there

I saw a crow by Red Rock
    standing on one leg
It was the black of your hair
    The years are heavy
I will ride the swiftest horse
You will hear the drumming hooves.

N. Scott Momaday

3

ARKANSAS

Walking after Supper
for Howard Nemerov

It is when I have thought of the universe
expanding until an atom becomes the size
of a solar system and millions of years pass
during the forming of a single thought,
of some place where gigantic young are taught
that we were here (though this will be known
by no evidence but logic alone,
all signs of us, and even our sun, gone),
that I have sometimes had to remind myself
that, say, if in a car at a crosswalk
a woman waves for me to go ahead,
this act deserves attention: that her doing that
equals in gravity all that has ever been
or will have been when we and the sun are dead.
All this I think in Fayetteville, Arkansas,
frozen here on the curb, in love, in awe.

Miller Williams

4

CALIFORNIA

The Changing Light

The changing light
                at San Francisco
        is none of your East Coast light
                none of your
                                pearly light of Paris
The light of San Francisco
                is a sea light
                                an island light
And the light of fog
                blanketing the hills
        drifting in at night
                through the Golden Gate
                                to lie on the city at dawn
And then the halcyon late mornings
        after the fog burns off
                and the sun paints white houses
                                with the sea light of Greece
                with sharp clean shadows
                        making the town look like
                                it had just been painted
But the wind comes up at four o'clock
                                sweeping the hills
And then the veil of light of early evening

And then another scrim
                when the new night fog
                                floats in
And in that vale of light
                the city drifts
                                anchorless upon the ocean

                                Lawrence Ferlinghetti

5

How Everything Was in the End Resolved in California

it
wasn't
san
andreas
fault
it
wasn't
mine
things
just
started
sliding.

Charles Foster

Seaweeds

This is the farthest out in the Sound I'll ever be,
the ebb tide so low I've walked a quarter mile
of sand flats rippling on and on like washboards
laid end to end. The waves are puppies rolling
over, lapping with blind eyes, gentle
and tender. You forget how large they'll grow,
how sloppy and brutal they can be. Like gardens,
the seaweeds wash to and fro, shining clean
you can almost taste them fresh rinsed
in your mouth. As many greens as on this shore:
lettuce green, early asparagus, dark steamed
artichoke, a bracken glow as if sea
water grows colors brighter than air. I wonder
about the mermaid child who'd wanted the world
in air and stone, who'd left her bull kelp forests,
golden climbers, swollen purple pods
for the raw rough bark of conifers and eucalyptus,
Weeds is not what I would call these limpid grasses
and broad dulses. Sugar wrack, grapestone, bulbous
and tufted, stringy, tubular, streamers,
fungiform, multiform, a sea of diversity
as lavish as on land. But I cannot walk

these flats endlessly. I must turn back
and face the new houses built to look out
to the Pacific. I have counted twelve flags
streaming on the late August air drafts,
a thirteenth almost too small for myopic eyes
to note in the distance, and who knows how many
more, flags that flap or hang or fly, forbidding
and uniform. Seaweeds, green and brown, gripping
onto their holdfasts of shell and stone,
drift slowly, wave with the incoming tide.
Today I have said good-bye to my son,
let him go onto this shore of flags and gardens.

                              Shirley Geok-lin Lim

COLORADO

Spirit that Form'd this Scene
Written in Platte Cañon, Colorado

Spirit that form'd this scene,
These tumbled rock-piles grim and red,
These reckless heaven-ambitious peaks,
These gorges, turbulent-clear streams, this naked freshness,

These formless wild arrays, for reasons of their own,
I know thee, savage spirit—we have communed together,
Mine too such wild arrays, for reasons of their own;
Was't charged against my chants they had forgotten art?
To fuse within themselves its rules precise and delicatesse?
The lyrist's measur'd beat, the wrought-out temple's
     grace—column and polish'd arch forgot?
But thou that revelest here—spirit that form'd this scene,
They have remember'd thee.

Walt Whitman

CONNECTICUT

The Hills of Little Cornwall

The hills of little Cornwall
Themselves are dreams.
The mind lies down among them,
Even by day, and snores,
Snug in the perilous knowledge
That nothing more inward pleasing,
More like itself,
Sleeps anywhere beyond them
Even by night
In the great land it cares two pins about,
Possibly; not more.

The mind, eager for caresses,
Lies down at its own risk in Cornwall;
Whose hills,
Whose cunning streams,
Whose mazes where a thought,
Doubling upon itself,
Considers the way, lazily, well lost,
Indulge it to the nick of death—
Not quite, for where it curls it still can feel,
Like feathers,
Like affectionate mouse whiskers,
The flattery, the trap.

Mark Van Doren

DELAWARE

A Few Lines from Rehoboth Beach

Dear friend, you were right: the smell of fish and foam
and algae makes one green smell together. It clears
my head. It empties me enough to fit down in my own

skin for a while, singleminded as a surfer. The first
day here, there was nobody, from one distance
to the other. Rain rose from the waves like steam,

dark lifted off the dark. All I could think of
were hymns, all I knew the words to: the oldest
motions tuning up in me. There was a horseshoe crab

shell, a translucent egg sack, a log of a tired jetty,
and another, and another. I walked miles, holding
my suffering deeply and courteously, as if I were holding

a package for somebody else who would come back
like sunlight. In the morning, the boardwalk opened
wide and white with sun, gulls on one leg in the slicks.

Cold waves, cold air, and people out in heavy coats,
arm in arm along the sheen of waves. A single boy
in shorts rode his skimboard out thigh-high, making

intricate moves across the March ice-water. I thought
he must be painfully cold, but, I hear you say, he had
all the world emptied, to practice his smooth stand.

Fleda Brown

FLORIDA

Nomad Exquisite

As the immense dew of Florida
Brings forth
The big-finned palm
And green vine angering for life,

As the immense dew of Florida
Brings forth hymn and hymn
From the beholder,
Beholding all these green sides
And gold sides of green sides,

And blessed mornings,
Meet for the eye of the young alligator,
And lightning colors
So, in me, come flinging
Forms, flames, and the flakes of flames.

Wallace Stevens

GEORGIA

Nocturne: Georgia Coast

The shrimping boats are late today;
The dusk has caught them cold.
Swift darkness gathers up the sun,
And all the beckoning gold
That guides them safely into port
Is lost beneath the tide.
Now the lean moon swings overhead,
And Venus, salty-eyed.

They will be late an hour or more,
The fishermen, blaming dark's
Swift mischief or the stubborn sea,
But as their lanterns' sparks
Ride shoreward at the foam's white rim,
Until they reach the pier
I cannot say if their catch is shrimp,
Or fireflies burning clear.

Daniel Whitehead Hicky

HAWAII

Silverswords

At cold daybreak
we wind
up the mountainside
to Haleakala Crater.
Our hands knot
under the rough of
your old army blanket.

We pass protea
and carnation farms
in Kula,
drive through
desolate rockfields.

Upon this one place
on Earth,
from the ancient
lava rivers,
silverswords rise,
startled
into starbursts
by the sun.
Like love, sometimes,
they die
at their first
and rare flowering.

Juliet Kono

13

IDAHO

Idaho Requiem
for Robert Lowell

Out here, we don't talk about culture,
we think we are. We nurtured Ezra Pound
who ran from us like hell
and never came back. You
never came at all. You
will never know how clever
we never are out here.
You never drank red beer.
You never popped a grouse
under a blue spruce just because it was there.

Tell us about Schopenhauer and your friends
and fine old family. We left ours
at the Mississippi, have no names left
to drop. We spend our time
avoiding Californians and waiting
for the sage to bloom, and when it does
we miss the damn things half the time.
When a stranger comes in we smile
and say, "Tell us about yourself."
Then we listen real close.

But you would say, "I've said what I have to say."
Too subtle, perhaps, for a can of beer,
too Augustan for the Snake River breaks.
But how do you know this wasn't just
the place to die? Why not have those
kinfolk ship your bones out here, just
for irony's sake? We keep things plain
and clear because of the mountains.
Our mythology comes down to a logger
stirring his coffee with his thumb.

Ron McFarland

14

ILLINOIS

Chicago

Hog Butcher for the World,
Tool Maker, Stacker of Wheat,
Player with Railroads and the Nation's Freight Handler;
Stormy, husky, brawling,
City of the Big Shoulders:

They tell me you are wicked and I believe them, for I have seen
your painted women under the gas lamps luring the farm boys.
And they tell me you are crooked and I answer: Yes, it is true I have
seen the gunman kill and go free to kill again.
And they tell me you are brutal and my reply is: On the faces of
women and children I have seen the marks of wanton hunger.
And having answered so I turn once more to those who sneer at this
my city, and I give them back the sneer and say to them:
Come and show me another city with lifted head singing so proud
to be alive and coarse and strong and cunning.
Flinging magnetic curses amid the toil of piling job on job, here is a
tall bold slugger set vivid against the little soft cities;
Fierce as a dog with tongue lapping for action, cunning as a savage
pitted against the wilderness,
    Bareheaded,
    Shoveling,
    Wrecking,
    Planning,
    Building, breaking, rebuilding,
Under the smoke, dust all over his mouth, laughing with white teeth,
Under the terrible burden of destiny laughing as a young man laughs,
Laughing even as an ignorant fighter laughs who has never lost a
battle,

Bragging and laughing that under his wrist is the pulse, and under
his ribs the heart of the people,
    Laughing!
Laughing the stormy, husky, brawling laughter of Youth, half-
naked, sweating, proud to be Hog Butcher, Tool Maker, Stacker
of Wheat, Player with Railroads and Freight Handler to the
Nation.

Carl Sandburg

INDIANA

July in Indiana

The wispy cuttings lie in rows
                     where mowers passed in the heat.
A parching scent enters the nostrils.

Morning barely breathed before
                     noon mounted on tiers of maples,
fiery and still. The eye smarts.

Moisture starts on the back of the hand.

Gloss and chrome on burning cars fan out
cobwebby lightning over children
                     damp and flushed in the shade.

Over all the back yards, locusts
buzz like little sawmills in the trees,
                     or is the song ecstatic?—rising
rising until it gets tired and dies away.

Grass baking, prickling sweat, great blazing tree,
magical shadow and cicada song
                     recall
those heroes that in ancient days, reclining
on roots and hummocks, tossing pen-knives,
                     delved in earth's cool underworld
and lightly squeezed the black clot from the blade.

Evening came, will come with lucid stillness
                     printed by the distinct cricket
and, far off, by the freight cars' coupling clank.

                     A warm full moon will rise
out of the mothering dust, out of the dry corn land.

                               Robert Fitzgerald

IOWA

Iowa

It never completely gets dark on those back roads.
There are stars, deceptively few.
And velvet consumes and velvet erupts:
the softness is the leaves and the dirt paths and stables and skin. And eyes.

The dark places, the secret places: abrupt, always, fleeting
but indelibly there, like a muscle memory.
The ridiculous and impudent course of years means nothing:
the touch is the same, the taste. Iowa's sweet ground. I close my eyes to the
darkness and fall into it more and awake to the street disappearing into
fields and lost time.

A drive through the cemetery, a different place now
Winding up the hill marking a route in the dark with the pond
To stand breathless at the crest, arms wide open
I chart movements with a cartographer's conscience:
throw open my shirt and open my self to the sky flawed and stitched
        and whole
and welcome my mother and forgive my father and
know the slap shock of being born.

                                        Robbie Spilka Klein

KANSAS

Outside Abilene

the full rage of kansas
turns loose upon us.

On the mexican radio station
they are singing *Espiritu de mis sueños*
and that is
exactly it tonight.

The spirit of my dreams
rises in the storm like vapor.

Deep clouds bulge together
and below them
we are a tiny constellation of lights
the car
laid under sheets of lightning
moving straight in to the night.

Before us are miles
and miles of water and wind.

Harley Elliott

KENTUCKY

Kentucky River Junction
to Ken Kesey & Ken Babbs

Clumsy at first, fitting together
the years we have been apart,
and the ways.

But as the night
passed and the day came, the first
fine morning of April,

it came clear:
the world that has tried us
and showed us its joy

was our bond
when we said nothing.
And we allowed it to be

with us, the new green
shining.

•

Our lives, half gone,
stay full of laughter.

Free-hearted men
have the world for words.

Though we have been
apart, we have been together.

●

Trying to sleep, I cannot
take my mind away.
The bright day

shines in my head
like a coin
on the bed of a stream.

●

You left
your welcome.

Wendell Berry

LOUISIANA

In Louisiana

The long, gray moss that softly swings
   In solemn grandeur from the trees,
   Like mournful funeral draperies,—
A brown-winged bird that never sings.

A shallow, stagnant, inland sea,
   Where rank swamp grasses wave, and where
   A deadliness lurks in the air,—
A sere leaf falling silently.

The death-like calm on every hand,
   That one might deem it sin to break,
   So pure, so perfect,—these things make
The mournful beauty of this land.

Albert Bigelow Paine

MAINE

Marin

Marin
saw how it feels:
the first raw shock
of Labrador current,
the surfacing gasp
at jut of rock,
bent sails, and wedged
trees. He wrote it—
Stonington, Small
Point, and Cape Split—
through a pane so
cracked by the lode-
star sun that he
swam back, blinded,
into himself, to
sign the after-
image: initialled
mountains, ledged
towns white as
Machias after
the hayrake rain,
sun-splintered
water, and written
granite—dark light
unlike what you
ever saw, until,
inland, your own
eyes close and, out
of that sea change,
islands rise thick,

like the riptide
paint that, flooding,
tugs at your vitals,
and is more Maine
than Maine.

Philip Booth

MARYLAND

blessing the boats
(*at St. Mary's*)

may the tide
that is entering even now
the lip of our understanding
carry you out
beyond the face of fear
may you kiss
the wind then turn from it
certain that it will
love your back   may you
open your eyes to water
water waving forever
and may you in your innocence
sail through this to that

Lucille Clifton

MASSACHUSETTS

Coming Home

When we're driving, in the dark,
on the long road
to Provincetown, which lies empty
for miles, when we're weary,
when the buildings
and the scrub pines lose
their familiar look,
I imagine us rising
from the speeding car,
I imagine us seeing
everything from another place—the top
of one of the pale dunes
or the deep and nameless
fields of the sea—
and what we see is the world
that cannot cherish us
but which we cherish,
and what we see is our life
moving like that,
along the dark edges
of everything—the headlights
like lanterns
sweeping the blackness—
believing in a thousand
fragile and unprovable things,
looking out for sorrow,
slowing down for happiness,
making all the right turns
right down to the thumping

barriers to the sea,
the swirling waves,
the narrow streets, the houses,
the past, the future,
the doorway that belongs
to you and me.

Mary Oliver

MICHIGAN

Drum
Leo's Tool & Die, 1950

In the early morning before the shop
opens, men standing out in the yard
on pine planks over the umber mud.
The oil drum, squat, brooding, brimmed
with metal scraps, three-armed crosses,
silver shavings whitened with milky oil,
drill bits bitten off. The light diamonds
last night's rain; inside a buzzer purrs.
The overhead door stammers upward
to reveal the scene of our day.
                              We sit
for lunch on crates before the open door.
Bobeck, the boss's nephew, squats to hug
the overflowing drum, gasps and lifts. Rain
comes down in sheets staining his gun-metal
covert suit. A stake truck sloshes off
as the sun returns through a low sky.
By four the office help has driven off. We
sweep, wash up, punch out, collect outside
for a final smoke. The great door crashes
down at last.
                    In the darkness the scents
of mint, apples, asters. In the darkness
this could be a Carthaginian outpost sent
to guard the waters of the West, those mounds
could be elephants at rest, the acrid half light
the haze of stars striking armor if stars were out.
On the galvanized tin roof the tunes of sudden rain.

The slow light of Friday morning in Michigan,
the one we waited for, shows seven hills
of scraped earth topped with crab grass,
weeds, a black oil drum empty, glistening
at the exact center of the modern world.

Philip Levine

MINNESOTA

A Blessing

Just off the highway to Rochester, Minnesota,
Twilight bounds softly forth on the grass.
And the eyes of those two Indian ponies
Darken with kindness.
They have come gladly out of the willows
To welcome my friend and me.
We step over the barbed wire into that pasture
Where they have been grazing all day, alone.
They ripple tensely, they can hardly contain their happiness
That we have come.
They bow shyly as wet swans. They love each other.
There is no loneliness like theirs.
At home once more,
They begin munching the young tufts of spring in the darkness.
I would like to hold the slenderer one in my arms,
For she has walked over to me
And nuzzled my left hand.
She is black and white,
Her mane falls wild on her forehead,
And the light breeze moves me to caress her long ear
That is delicate as the skin over a girl's wrist.
Suddenly I realize
That if I stepped out of my body I would break
Into blossom.

James Wright

MISSISSIPPI

On the Mississippi

Through wild and tangled forests
  The broad, unhasting river flows—
    Spotted with rain-drops, gray with night;
      Upon its curving breast there goes
A lonely steamboat's larboard light,
      A blood-red star against the shadowy oaks;
Noiseless as a ghost, through greenish gleam
Of fire-flies, before the boat's wild scream—
      A heron flaps away
      Like silence taking flight.

Hamlin Garland

MISSOURI

Found Poem
after information received
in The St. Louis Post-Dispatch
4 v 86

The population center of the USA
Has shifted to Potosi, in Missouri.

The calculation employed by authorities
In arriving at this dislocation assumes

That the country is a geometric plane,
Perfectly flat, and that every citizen,

Including those in Alaska and Hawaii
And the District of Columbia, weighs the same;

So that, given these simple presuppositions,
The entire bulk and spread of all the people

Should theoretically balance on the point
Of a needle under Potosi in Missouri

Where no one is residing nowadays
But the watchman over an abandoned mine

Whence the company got the lead out and left.
"It gets pretty lonely here," he says, "at night."

Howard Nemerov

MONTANA

Once in the 40s

We were alone one night on a long
road in Montana. This was in winter, a big
night, far to the stars. We had hitched,
my wife and I, and left our ride at
a crossing to go on. Tired and cold—but
brave—we trudged along. This, we said,
was our life, watched over, allowed to go
where we wanted. We said we'd come back some time
when we got rich. We'd leave the others and find
a night like this, whatever we had to give,
and no matter how far, to be so happy again.

William Stafford

NEBRASKA

Prairie Spring

Evening and the flat land,
Rich and somber and always silent;
The miles of fresh-plowed soil,
Heavy and black, full of strength and harshness;
The growing wheat, the growing weeds,
The toiling horses, the tired men;
The long, empty roads,
Sullen fires of sunset, fading,
The eternal, unresponsive sky.
Against all this, Youth,
Flaming like the wild roses,
Singing like the larks over the plowed fields,
Flashing like a star out of the twilight;
Youth with its unsupportable sweetness,
Its fierce necessity,
Its sharp desire;
Singing and singing,
Out of the lips of silence
Out of the earthy dusk.

Willa Cather

NEVADA

driving to Vegas

Tonopah's
the only place
contour lines
appear
to rise

between there
and Goldfield
the first
Joshua trees

beer at the Mozart Club

from then on
it's all downhill

between Mercury
and Indian Springs
the light
begins to change

you wonder
what you'll do
when you reach
the edge
of the map

out there
on the horizon

all that neon

beckoning you

in from the dark

Kirk Robertson

NEW HAMPSHIRE

Stopping by Woods on a Snowy Evening
from New Hampshire Poems

Whose woods these are I think I know.
His house is in the village, though;
He will not see me stopping here
To watch his woods fill up with snow.

My little horse must think it queer
To stop without a farmhouse near
Between the woods and frozen lake
The darkest evening of the year.

He gives his harness bells a shake
To ask if there is some mistake.
The only other sound's the sweep
Of easy wind and downy flake.

The woods are lovely, dark and deep,
But I have promises to keep,
And miles to go before I sleep,
And miles to go before I sleep.

Robert Frost

NEW JERSEY

Night Driving

South into Jersey on I-95 rain and
windshield wipers and someone you love asleep
in the seat beside you, light on all sides
like teeth winking and that smell like baking
bread gone wrong and you want
to die it's so beautiful—
you love the enormous trucks floating in spray
and the tall smokestacks rimmed with flame
and this hammering in your head
this magnet drawing what's deepest
in you you can't name
except to know it's there.

Joyce Carol Oates

NEW MEXICO

Passing through Albuquerque

At dusk, by the irrigation ditch
gurgling past backyards near the highway,
locusts raise a maze of calls in cottonwoods.

A Spanish girl in a white party dress
strolls the levee by the muddy water
where her small sister plunks in stones.

Beyond a low adobe wall and a wrecked car
men are pitching horseshoes in a dusty lot.
Someone shouts as he clangs in a ringer.

Big winds buffet in ahead of a storm,
rocking the immense trees and whipping up
clouds of dust, wild leaves, and cottonwool.

In the moment when the locusts pause and the girl
presses her up-fluttering dress to her bony knees
you can hear a banjo, guitar, and fiddle

playing "The Mississippi Sawyer" inside a shack.
Moments like that, you can love this country.

John Balaban

NEW YORK

Just a New York Poem

i wanted to take
your hand and run with you
together toward
ourselves down the street to your street
i wanted to laugh aloud
and skip the notes past
the marquee advertising "women
in love" past the record
shop with "The Spirit
In The Dark" past the smoke shop
past the park and no
parking today signs
past the people watching me in
my blue velvet and i don't remember
what you wore but only that i didn't want
anything to be wearing you
i wanted to give
myself to the cyclone that is
your arms
and let you in the eye of my hurricane and know
the calm before

and some fall evening
after the cocktails
and the very expensive and very bad
steak served with day-old baked potatoes
and the second cup of coffee taken
while listening to the rejected

violin player
maybe some fall evening
when the taxis have passed you by
and that light sort of rain
that occasionally falls
in new york begins
you'll take a thought
and laugh aloud
the notes carrying all the way over
to me and we'll run again
together
toward each other
yes?

                                        Nikki Giovanni

Long Island Sound

I see it as it looked one afternoon
In August,—by a fresh soft breeze o'erblown.
The swiftness of the tide, the light thereon,
A far-off sail, white as a crescent moon.
The shining waters with pale currents strewn,
The quiet fishing-smacks, the Eastern cove,
The semi-circle of its dark, green grove.
The luminous grasses, and the merry sun
In the grave sky; the sparkle far and wide,
Laughter of unseen children, cheerful chirp
Of crickets, and low lisp of rippling tide,
Light summer clouds fantastical as sleep
Changing unnoted while I gazed thereon.
All these fair sounds and sights I made my own.

                                        Emma Lazarus

NORTH CAROLINA

From **Mountain Time**

Up here in the mountains
we know what extinct means. We've seen
how our breath on a bitter night
fades like a ghost from the window glass.
We know the wolf's gone.
The panther. We've heard the old stories
run down, stutter out
into silence. Who knows where we're heading?
All roads seem to lead
to Millennium, dark roads with drop-offs
we can't plumb. It's time to be brought up short
now with the tale-tellers' Listen: There once lived
a woman named Delphia
who walked through these hills teaching children
to read. She was known as a quilter
whose hand never wearied, a mother
who raised up two daughters to pass on
her words like a strong chain of stitches.
Imagine her sitting among us,
her quick thimble moving along these lines
as if to hear every word striking true
as the stab of her needle through calico.
While prophets discourse about endings,
don't you think she'd tell us the world as we know it
keeps calling us back to beginnings?
This labor to make our words matter
is what any good quilter teaches.
A stitch in time, let's say.

A blind stitch
that clings to the edges
of what's left, the ripped
scraps and remnants, whatever
won't stop taking shape even though the whole
crazy quilt's falling to pieces.

Kathryn Stripling Byer

NORTH DAKOTA

Early Cutting
For Ed Elderman

When they take the winter wheat at home
all the other crops are green.
In granaries and tight truck boxes
farm boys are slow scoop-shovel metronomes
singing harvest deep in the grain.

The old men come out to watch, squat in the stubble,
break a lump of dirt and look at it on their hands,
and mumbling kernels of the sweet hard durum,
they think how it survived the frozen ground
unwinding at last to this perfect bread
of their mouths.

Where they call it the Red River Valley of the North
there are no mountains,
the floor is wide as a glacial lake—Agassiz,
the fields go steady to the horizon,
sunflower, potato, summerfallow, corn,
and so flat that a shallow ditch
can make tractor drivers think of Columbus
and the edge.

Roland Flint

OHIO

A Walk Along the Old Tracks

When I was young they had already been
abandoned for years
overgrown with sumac and sour apple,
the iron scrapped, the wood long
gone for other things.
In summer my father would send us along them
to fetch the cows from the back pasture,
a long walk to a far off place it seemed
for boys so young. Lost again for a moment
in that simple place,
I fling apples from a stick and look for snakes
in the gullies. There is
a music to the past, the sweet tones
of perfect octaves
even though we know it was never so.
My father had to sell the farm in that near perfect time
and once old Al Shott killed a six foot rattler on the tracks.
"And when the trolly was running" he said, "you could jump
her as she went by and ride all the way to Cleveland,
and oh," he said, "what a time you could have there."

Robert Kinsley

OKLAHOMA

Grandfather's Song

The Osage family moved slowly to the beat,
circling the drum with sons and daughters,
grandchildren and great-grandchildren.
Friends joined behind and beside.
We outside the dance stood quiet,
solemn as the dancers in tribute.
To have a song with Grandfather's name,
a tribute for a whole tribe to know,
respect for those now our memories—
we should learn from this pride.

My grandfather's song will have the rhythm
of train wheels on tracks, slow
regular, climbing long slopes.
It will dip and cry like the whistle
of steam rising over the valley,
sharp as red leaves on a mountainside.
Word sounds will jumble and roll
like the voices of many children calling,
playing homemade games of older days.
And in the end it will settle soft,
with the screaking click of a rocker
on a wood porch and tall hemlocks sighing, quiet
as the slow breath of an old man, remembering.

Let us, too, make songs of honor so our old men
are never quite gone.

Nan Arbuckle

OREGON

Oregon Winter

The rain begins. This is no summer rain,
Dropping the blotches of wet on the dusty road:
This rain is slow, without thunder or hurry:
There is plenty of time—there will be months of rain.
   Lost in the hills, the old gray farmhouses
Hump their backs against it, and smoke from their chimneys
Struggles through weighted air. The sky is sodden with water,
It sags against the hills, and the wild geese,
Wedge-flying, brush the heaviest cloud with their wings.
   The farmers move unhurried. The wood is in,
The hay has long been in, the barn lofts piled
Up to the high windows, dripping yellow straws.
There will be plenty of time now, time that will smell of fires,
And drying leather, and catalogues, and apple cores.
   The farmers clean their boots, and whittle, and drowse.

Jeanne Mc Gahey

PENNSYLVANIA

Fishing on the Susquehanna in July

I have never been fishing on the Susquehanna
or on any river for that matter
to be perfectly honest.

Not in July or any month
have I had the pleasure—if it is a pleasure—
of fishing on the Susquehanna.

I am more likely to be found
in a quiet room like this one—
a painting of a woman on the wall,

a bowl of tangerines on the table—
trying to manufacture the sensation
of fishing on the Susquehanna.

There is little doubt
that others have been fishing
on the Susquehanna,

rowing upstream in a wooden boat,
sliding the oars under the water
then raising them to drip in the light.

But the nearest I have ever come to
fishing on the Susquehanna
was one afternoon in a museum in Philadelphia

when I balanced a little egg of time
in front of a painting
in which that river curled around a bend

under a blue cloud-ruffled sky,
dense trees along the banks,
and a fellow with a red bandanna

sitting in a small, green
flat-bottom boat
holding the thin whip of a pole.

That is something I am unlikely
ever to do, I remember
saying to myself and the person next to me.

Then I blinked and moved on
to other American scenes
of haystacks, water whitening over rocks,

even one of a brown hare
who seemed so wired with alertness
I imagined him springing right out of the frame.

                                          Billy Collins

RHODE ISLAND

Jerimoth Hill
812 feet, the highest point in Rhode Island

You will not recognize any bald knob of granite
or sheer cliff face silhouetted against clouds,
in fact, you won't realize you're anywhere at all
except by this bullet-riddled sign by the road
that curves through these scraggled third growth
woods that was once a grove of giant pines
that were cut down for masts that were used
to build ships to sail away to the rest of the world
from the docks of Providence Harbor, their holds
filled with wool from the sheep that grazed
in the field that had once been the giant pines
till the shepherds died off and the applers took over
and grew orchards of Cortlands and Macintosh
Delicious to fill the holds of the ships that sailed
to the rest of the world from the docks of Providence
Harbor with masts made from the giant pines till
the orchards moved west along with everything
else to less glacial land and the fields became
overgrowth of berries and hobblebush crisscrossed
by walls made of stones that had slept beneath
one inch of topsoil for twelve thousand years
till the settlers found when they tried to plant crops
that this was a country that grew only rocks which
they made into walls to pen in the sheep that provided
the wool that filled the holds of the ships that sailed
to the rest of the world from the docks of Providence Harbor.

Tom Chandler

SOUTH CAROLINA

At the Public Market Museum:
Charleston, South Carolina

A volunteer, a Daughter of the Confederacy,
receives my admission and points the way.
Here are gray jackets with holes in them,
red sashes with individual flourishes,
things soft as flesh. Someone sewed
the gold silk cord onto that gray sleeve
as if embellishments
could keep a man alive.

I have been reading *War and Peace*,
and so the particulars of combat
are on my mind—the shouts and groans
of men and boys, and the horses' cries
as they fall, astonished at what
has happened to them.   Blood on leaves,
blood on grass, on snow; extravagant
beauty of red. Smoke, dust of disturbed
earth; parch and burn.

Who would choose this for himself?
And yet the terrible machinery
waited in place. With psalters
in their breast pockets, and gloves
knitted by their sisters and sweethearts,
the men in gray hurled themselves
out of the trenches, and rushed against
blue. It was what both sides
agreed to do.

                                   Jane Kenyon

SOUTH DAKOTA

Dakota: Five Times Six

Nobody painted Mrs. Aherne's store
And, standing at a corner where dry wind
Sanded it, all its boards turned bone-gray finally,
And by the time I visited, untended,
The barbershop next door—where Mr. Mack
Told jokes I smiled at, fearing all the while
The flyspecked Lucky Tiger on the wall,
Out of the corner of my six year's eye—
I could remember it no other color.

I can remember now, at five times six,
Her dress—beyond the crystal candy jars,
Behind the smeary counter glass—was gray
(Dyed gray, maybe, not weathered, but gray as
The siding of her store); so were her hair
And eyes, even the tarnished silver brooch
That pinched her dress tight at the withered throat.

Dakota six knew bone-gray when he saw it:
Cows often died in fields of only dust,
So did farmhouses with their eyes poked out.
I can remember bone-gray, bleached-board gray
Better than rainbows—there it seldom rained.

But Mrs. Aherne sold taste rainbows at
Two for one cent, and from her shelves rained sugar.

Joseph Hansen

TENNESSEE

Tenantry
(Polk County, Tennessee)

Always in transit
we were always temporarily
in exile,
each new place seeming
after a while
and for a while
our home.

Because no matter
how far we traveled
on the edge of strangeness
in a small county,
the earth ran before us
down red clay roads
blurred with summer dust,
banked with winter mud.

It was the measurable,
pleasurable earth
that was home.
Nobody who loved it
could ever be really alien.
Its tough clay, deep loam,
hill rocks, small flowers
were always the signs
of a homecoming.

We wound down through them
to them,
and the house we came to,
whispering with dead hollyhocks
or once in spring
sill-high in daisies,
was unimportant.
Wherever it stood,
it stood in earth,

and the earth welcomed us,
open, gateless,
one place as another.
And each place seemed
after a while
and for a while
our home:
because the county
was only a mansion
kind of dwelling
in which there were many
rooms.
We only moved from one
room to another,
getting acquainted
with the whole house.

And always the earth
was the new floor under us,
the blue pinewoods the walls
rising around us,
the windows the openings
in the blue trees
through which we glimpsed,
always farther on,
sometimes beyond the river,
the real wall of the mountain,
in whose shadow
for a little while
we assumed ourselves safe,
secure and comfortable
as happy animals
in an unvisited lair:

which is why perhaps
no house we ever lived in
stood behind a fence,
no door we ever opened
had a key.

It was beautiful like that.
For a little while.

George Scarbrough

TEXAS

South Texas Summer Rain

Dust cools easily
with the lightest summer rain.
Not rocks.
In the midst of dry brush,
they hold the sun like a match,
a threat to the water
that would wear them out.

Dust becomes clay,
cups rain like an innocent offering.
Not rocks.

They round their backs to the rain,
channel it down the street where children play,
feeling the rocks they walk on,
sharp as ever under the water,
streaming away.

If rocks hold water at all,
it's only long enough
for a cactus to grow gaudy flowers,
hoard a cheap drink,
flash it like a sin
worth the pain.

Rebecca Gonzales

The Waltz We Were Born For

I never knew them all, just hummed
and thrummed my fingers with the radio,
driving five hundred miles to Austin.
Her arms held all the songs I needed.
Our boots kept time with fiddles
and the charming sobs of blondes,

the whine of steel guitars
sliding us down in deer-hide chairs
when jukebox music was over.
Sad music's on my mind tonight
in a jet high over Dallas, earphones
on channel five. A lonely singer,

dead, comes back to beg me,
swearing in my ears she's mine,
rhymes set to music that make
her lies seem true. She's gone
and others like her, leaving their songs
to haunt us. Letting down through clouds

I know who I'll find waiting at the gate,
the same woman faithful to my arms
as she was those nights in Austin
when the world seemed like a jukebox,
our boots able to dance forever,
our pockets full of coins.

                                        Walt McDonald

UTAH

Spring
from **To Utah**

Spring came slowly to the valley lands,
Slower to the hills
Where pines unmortised from their melting molds
Slipped dripping loads,
And their glistening needles, wetwaxed, glared.
Ice on the creek
Quit cracking, crashing caves of crystals,
Soon resumed
The rumble and the rush of far-off feud.
A dark town
Cowered in the canyon mouth between
The hills' knees.
Its bare trees bristling like a ruffled bird's
Plumes. The all
But inaudible sound of the sinking snow
Stirred wonder without words
In us. We forsook the long wan winter's
Bound encumbrance
And felt the unfettered freedom of the live
Loadlifted limbs.

Edward L. Hart

VERMONT

The Cows at Night

The moon was like a full cup tonight,
too heavy, and sank in the mist
soon after dark, leaving for light

faint stars and the silver leaves
of milkweed beside the road,
gleaming before my car.

Yet I like driving at night
in summer and in Vermont:
the brown road through the mist

of mountain-dark, among farms
so quiet, and the roadside willows
opening out where I saw

the cows. Always a shock
to remember them there, those
great breathings close in the dark.

I stopped, taking my flashlight
to the pasture fence. They turned
to me where they lay, sad

and beautiful faces in the dark,
and I counted them—forty
near and far in the pasture,

turning to me, sad and beautiful
like girls very long ago
who were innocent, and sad

because they were innocent,
and beautiful because they were
sad. I switched off my light.

But I did not want to go,
not yet, nor knew what to do
if I should stay, for how

in that great darkness could I explain
anything, anything at all.
I stood by the fence. And then

very gently it began to rain.

Hayden Carruth

VIRGINIA

Virginia Evening

Just past dusk I passed Christiansburg,
cluster of lights sharpening
as the violet backdrop of the Blue Ridge
darkened. Not stars
but blue-black mountains rose
before me, rose like sleep
after hours of driving, hundreds of miles
blurred behind me. My eyelids
were so heavy but I could see
far ahead a summer thunderstorm flashing,
lightning sparking from cloud
to mountaintop. I drove toward it,
into the pass at Ironto, the dark
now deeper in the long steep grades,
heavy in the shadow of mountains weighted
with evergreens, with spruce, pine,
and cedar. How I wished to sleep
in that sweet air, which filled—
suddenly over a rise—with the small
lights of countless fireflies. Everywhere
they drifted, sweeping from the trees
down to the highway my headlights lit.
Fireflies blinked in the distance
and before my eyes, just before
the windshield struck them and they died.
Cold phosphorescent green, on the glass
their bodies clung like buds bursting
the clean line of a branch in spring.

How long it lasted, how many struck
and bloomed as I drove on, hypnotic
stare fixed on the road ahead, I can't say.
Beyond them, beyond their swarming
bright deaths came the rain, a shower
which fell like some dark blessing.
Imagine when I flicked the windshield wipers on
what an eerie glowing beauty faced me.
In that smeared, streaked light
diminished sweep by sweep you could have seen
my face. It was weary, shocked, awakened,
alive with wonder far after the blades and rain
swept clean the light of those lives
passed, like stars rolling over
the earth, now into other lives.

Michael Pettit

WASHINGTON

Mid-August at Sourdough Mountain Lookout

Down valley a smoke haze
Three days heat, after five days rain
Pitch glows on the fir-cones
Across rocks and meadows
Swarms of new flies.

I cannot remember things I once read
A few friends, but they are in cities.
Drinking cold snow-water from a tin cup
Looking down for miles
Through high still air.

Gary Snyder

WASHINGTON, D.C

From The Congressional Library

Where else in all America are we so symbolized
As in this hall?
White columns polished like glass,
A dome and a dome,
A balcony and a balcony,
Stairs and the balustrades to them,
Yellow marble and red slabs of it,
All mounting, spearing, flying into color.
Color round the dome and up to it,
Color curving, kite-flying, to the second dome,
Light, dropping, pitching down upon the color,
Arrow-falling upon the glass-bright pillars,
Mingled colors spinning into a shape of white pillars,
Fusing, cooling, into balanced shafts of shrill and interthronging light.
This is America,
This vast, confused beauty,
This staring, restless speed of loveliness,
Mighty, overwhelming, crude, of all forms,
Making grandeur out of profusion,
Afraid of no incongruities,
Sublime in its audacity,
Bizarre breaker of moulds,
Laughing with strength,
Charging down on the past,
Glorious and conquering,
Destroyer, builder,
Invincible pith and marrow of the world,
An old world remaking,
Whirling into the no-world of all-colored light.

Amy Lowell

WEST VIRGINIA

Appalachian Front

Panther lies next to Wharncliffe
and Wharncliffe next to Devon
and Devon next to Delorme.
In each a single fisherman casts
in the slow, black water of the Big Sandy.
Catfish is the whisker lurking
behind the bobbing cork.
He lives, it seems, in dense night
from day to day until the fisherman
from Wharncliffe pulls him out
to be fried in tin-roof, tarpaper shacks
from there to Matewan.

Politicians call this valley
a depressed area.
But, under the sun, my heart
will not have it so.
Straight up from the brackish water,
up the mountainside, green pointed trees
as close as bird's wings
grow fierce and clean,
and then for miles beside the tracks
the river moves faster over the rocks
and the water isn't black at all—
only the silt underneath.
The water over the rocks
is running clear and cold and pure.

Robert Lewis Weeks

WISCONSIN

From **For John Muir, A Century and More After His Time**

I have seen those Indians in their birch canoes,
Menominees, in shallow lake or stream,
Threshing their wild rice. Through Wisconsin haze
I see the water gleam,
                            the small craft tilt,
And through the clustering stems
The small waves lap upon the glacial silt,
As John Muir saw them, years and years ago.
Or do I use
A borrowed memory, learned in my childhood days
From my Ojibway friends?
                            All that Wisconsin scene,
Familiar as my breath, lives when I choose
To look upon his page:
The muskrat nibbling where the alders bend,
The water plants that gave it summer forage,
Great cumuli piled against thunderous blues
Of summer skies; hepatica and faint anemones
That come before the sunlit woods are leafy;
Bronzed oak and fiery maple, all the gold
Of harvest where the summer ends;
                            all these
In memory, both mine and borrowed, doubly rich
        are grown,
Till I can hardly tell his treasure from my own.

                                    Janet Lewis

WYOMING

Lupine Ridge

Long after we are gone,
Summer will stroke this ridge in blue;
The hawk still flies above the flowers,
Thinking, perhaps, the sky has fallen
And back and forth forever he may trace
His shadow on its azure face.

Long after we are gone,
Evening wind will languish here
Between the lupine and the sage
To die a little death upon the earth,
As though over the sundown prairies fell
A requiem from a bronze-tongued bell.

Long after we are gone,
This ridge will shape the night,
Lifting the wine-streaked west,
Shouldering the stars.   And always here
Lovers will walk under the summer skies
Through flowers the color of your eyes.

Peggy Simson Curry

Index of Titles